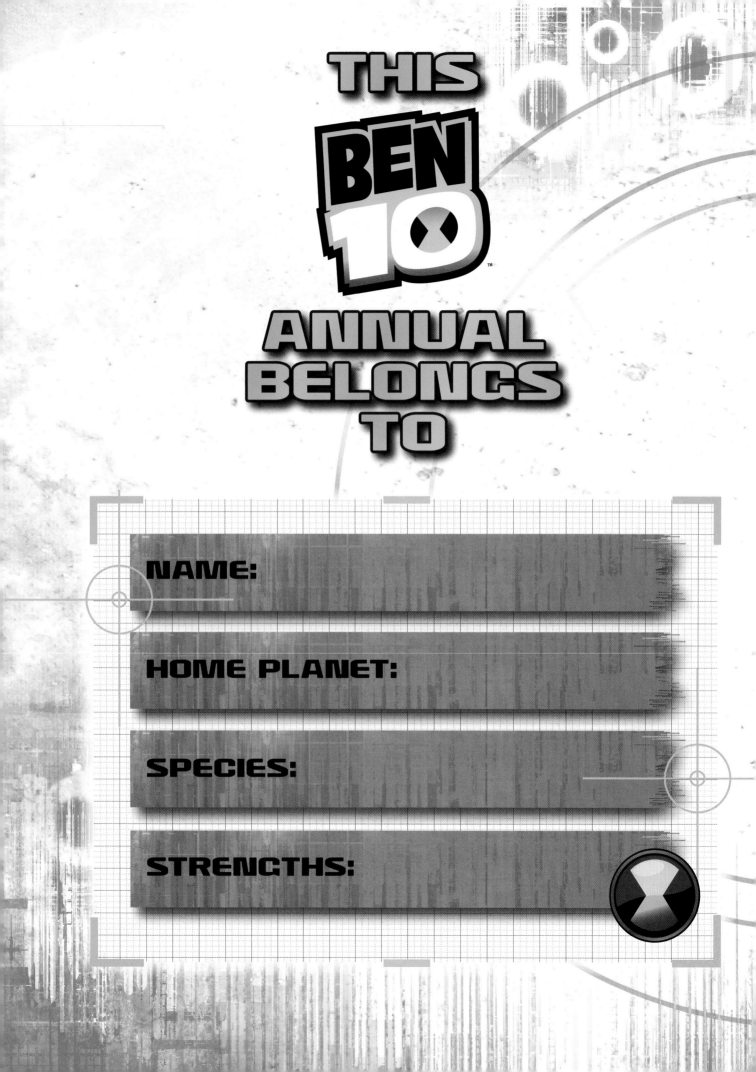

THIS BEN 10 ANNUAL BELONGS TO

NAME:

HOME PLANET:

SPECIES:

STRENGTHS:

CONTENTS

EGMONT

We bring stories to life

First published in Great Britain 2012 by Egmont UK Limited
239 Kensington High Street, London W8 6SA
Text by Laura Milne. Design by Ant Duke.

Cartoon Network, the logo, BEN 10 and all related characters and elements are trademarks of and © 2012 Cartoon Network.
All rights reserved.

ISBN 978 1 4052 6335 1
51508/1
Printed in Italy

No part of this publication may be reproduced, stored in a retrieval system, or transmitted in any form or by any means, electronic, mechanical, photocopying, recording or otherwise, without the prior permission of the publisher and copyright holder.

FIND JURYRIGG - He's tiny, but there are 10 hidden pictures of Juryrigg like this one throughout the book. Can you find them all?

Ben's out-of-this world adventure began when he was 10 years old. While he was on a summer trip with his Grandpa Max and cousin Gwen, a strange object from outer space crashed to Earth nearby. It turned out to be the Omnitrix, the watch-like gadget that allows Ben to turn into aliens to help save the world. And Ben's first alien transformation? It was the fiery Heatblast!

A few years have passed and, with the help of the even more powerful Ultimatrix, Ben's still turning alien to destroy villains intent on doing harm. It's a tall order, so Ben's glad to still have Gwen and Kevin – and their amazing powers – by his side. And Ben now has even more AWESOME aliens than ever!

So come and be reunited with some old friends and foes – and meet some new ones, too!

LET'S GO HERO!

BEN TENNYSON

Ben's had lots of practice turning alien over the years, but the villains are tough and saving the universe is hard work. Is Ben up for the challenge? You bet!

AGE: 16

LIKES: movies, games, being a superhero

DISLIKES: villains threatening his family and friends

Ben's own set of wheels – a very cool black and green sports car.

The original Omnitrix which allowed Ben to turn into ten incredible aliens!

The Ultimatrix – a new improved version of the Omnitrix. It can upgrade Ben's aliens into bigger, stronger beasts and can scan and store brand-new alien DNA.

HERO

GWEN TENNYSON

Gwen is Ben's cousin and a really good friend. She's the thinker of the group and also very brave. The granddaughter of an Anodite alien, Gwen has her own amazing powers.

AGE: 16

LIKES: her boyfriend Kevin, shopping, hanging out

DISLIKES: people acting before thinking

HERO

KEVIN LEVIN

Kevin knows how the bad guys operate – because he used to be one! Now one of the good guys, Kevin's an Osmosian who has the power to absorb any material he touches.

AGE: 17

LIKES: his girlfriend Gwen, his car, fighting bad guys

DISLIKES: being told what to do

9

FASTTRACK

Ben turns into Fasttrack when he needs super speed! Fasttrack is a cat-like alien with spikes on his arms and legs, and mask-like fins around his green eyes. Fasttrack is amazingly fast. He also has enhanced strength and is strong enough to carry heavy objects without losing any speed.

HERO

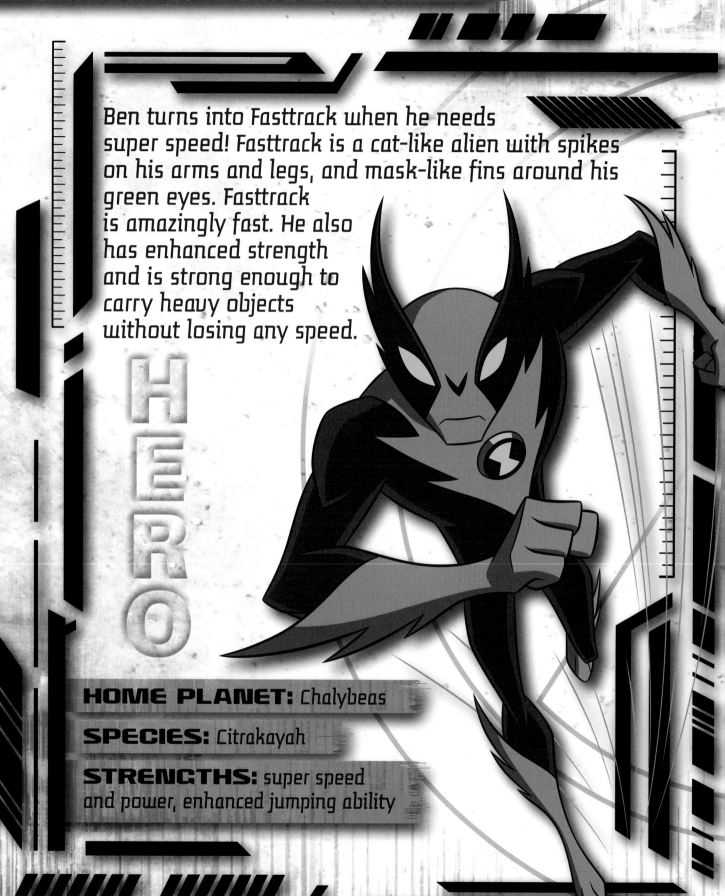

HOME PLANET: Chalybeas

SPECIES: Citrakayah

STRENGTHS: super speed and power, enhanced jumping ability

DANGER MAZE

Gwen is speeding off in Ben's car, with Aggregor and his drones in close pursuit. Ben turns into his lightning-fast alien, Fasttrack, to stop them. Help him through the maze to rescue Gwen!

START →

FINISH
→

CHAMALIEN

Just like a chameleon, ChamAlien can change the colour of his skin to become invisible – so Ben turns into him when he needs to be able to hide! ChamAlien looks a bit like a lizard, with camouflaged spots all over his body. He is incredibly agile and slippery, and can easily scale walls and ceilings.

HOME PLANET: unknown

SPECIES: Merlinisapien

STRENGTHS: camouflage, invisibility, a tail stinger, very strong and can climb walls

HERO

CHAMALIEN COUNT

ChamAlien is a master of disguise. How many times does he appear here? Write your answer below.

Which ChamAlien has different-coloured eyes?

JURYRIGG

Juryrigg is a small, devil-like alien, complete with a pointed tail and pointed ears. Ben turns into him when he needs to create mechanical mayhem! Juryrigg's abilities include being able to disassemble machines and reworking them to suit his needs or perform better. Juryrigg can also instantly teleport to different locations and generate smoke bombs for cover.

HOME PLANET: unknown

SPECIES: unknown

STRENGTHS: improving technology, teleportation, smoke bombs

SEEING DOTS

Juryrigg's come face-to-face with Aggregor. Who'll win this one-on-one match?

Play this game with a friend. Take it in turns to draw a line connecting any two dots – no diagonals allowed! Try to make a four-sided box. The player who completes the fourth side of the box can put their initial inside it, then draw a new line.

When there are no more dots left, count up the initials in each box. The player with the most boxes is the winner!

CLOCKWORK

A big and chunky robotic humanoid alien, Clockwork's tough body armour has a green circle on the front with what looks like gears and cogs inside – just like a clock. Clockwork has time-controlling powers and Ben turns into him whenever he wants to time travel. Clockwork can send others back in time, too!

HOME PLANET: unknown

SPECIES: unknown

STRENGTHS: time travel, can shoot time rays that send people back in time against their will

MOMENT IN TIME

Clockwork has been time travelling.
He's made 10 changes to the scene below.
Can you spot them all?

EATLE

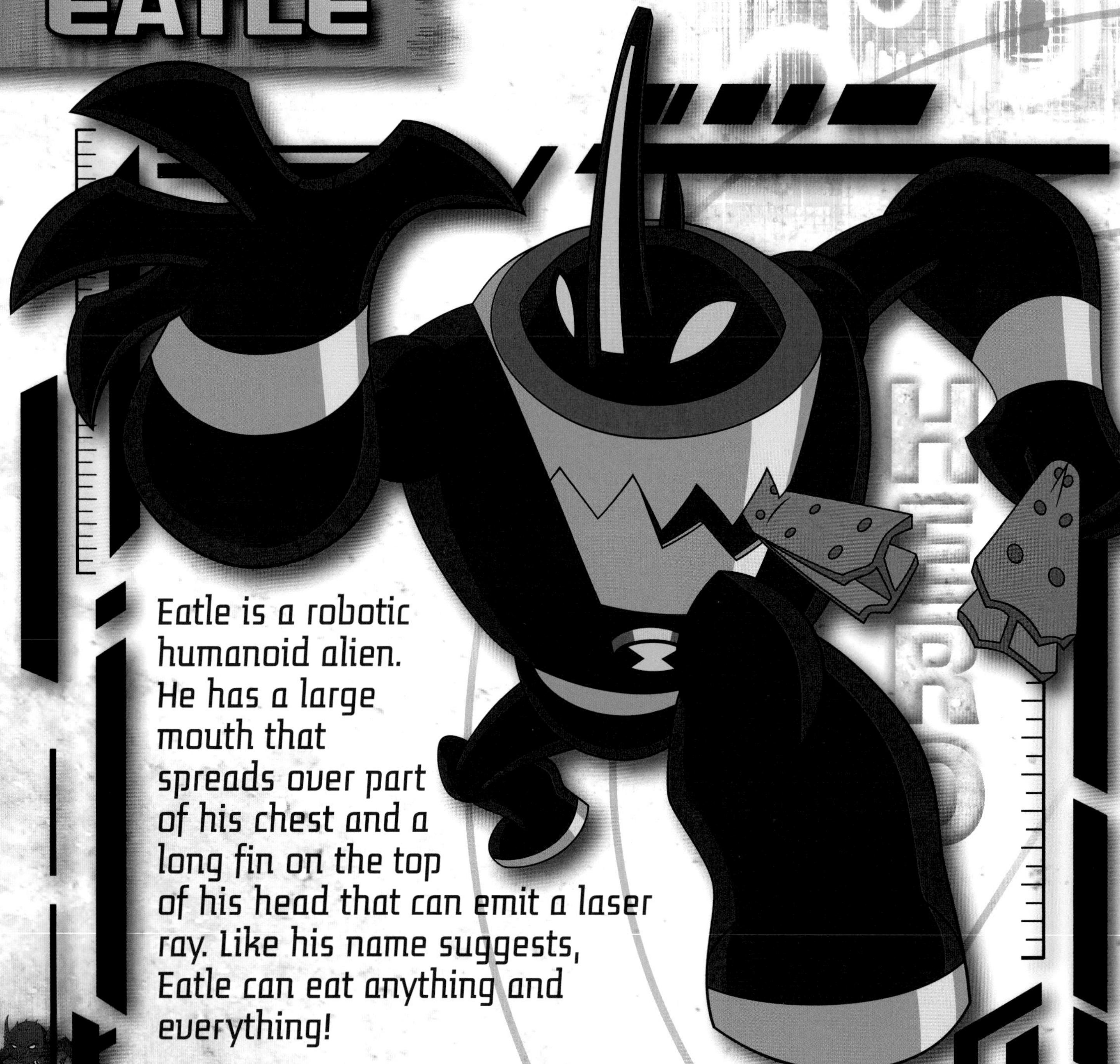

Eatle is a robotic humanoid alien. He has a large mouth that spreads over part of his chest and a long fin on the top of his head that can emit a laser ray. Like his name suggests, Eatle can eat anything and everything!

HOME PLANET: unknown

SPECIES: unknown

STRENGTHS: Can consume any material without harm, laser cutter beam, super power, razor claws

Starting with Eatle's chest and head, design your own awesome alien. Draw in whatever you like - arms, legs, wings or tail. Give him lots of colour!

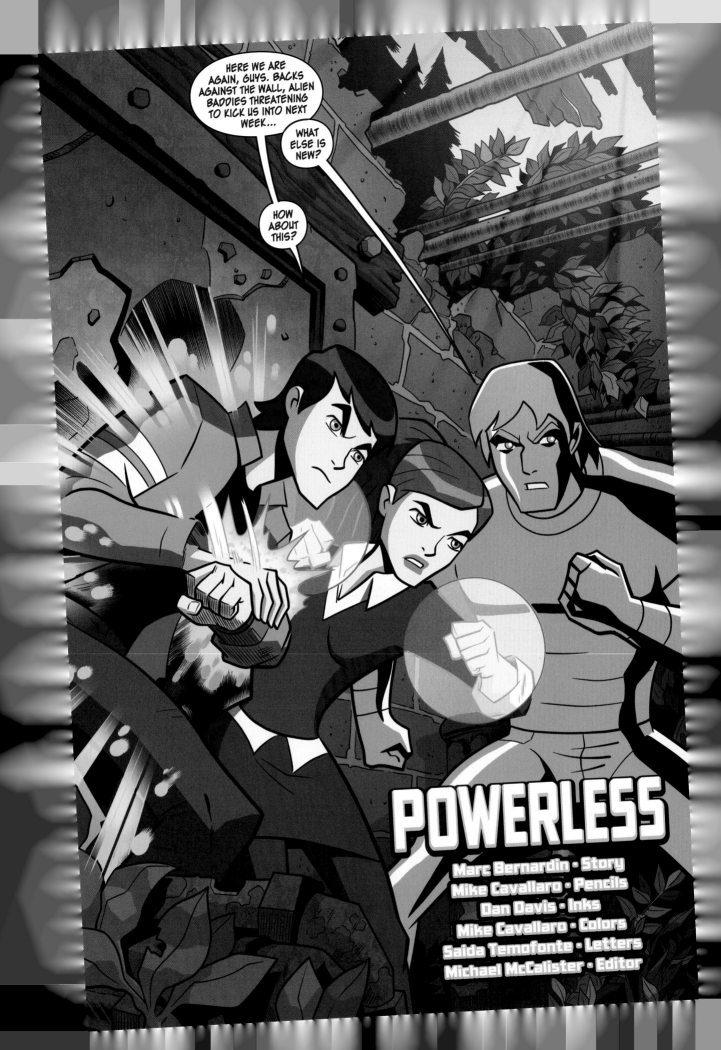

Continued on page 37 ...

Ultimate WILDMUTT

Ultimate Wildmutt is much larger and more muscular than Wildmutt – and angrier! He has spikes on his body, a tail, longer claws and sharper teeth.

FACT FILE

- Formed when Wildmutt hits his Omnitrix symbol
- His spiked tail is used as defence
- He is able to speak (unlike Wildmutt)

WILDMUTT

Ben first turned into Wildmutt when he was 10 years old. Wildmutt is a fast and vicious beast.

Ultimate SWAMPFIRE

Ultimate Swampfire's armour is made from bark. The bark consists of a gooey, highly flammable substance that he uses to create fire bombs.

FACT FILE

- Formed when Swampfire hits his Omnitrix symbol
- Incredibly tough
- Can create fire tornadoes

SWAMPFIRE

Swampfire is an extremely strong plant-like alien. He can regenerate himself and shoot fire.

Ultimate
SPIDERMONKEY

Ultimate Spidermonkey is a huge gorilla with nimble, long spider legs. He looks terrifying and can spit spider webs from his mouth!

FACT FILE

- Formed when Spidermonkey hits his Omnitrix symbol
- Immensely strong
- His webs are tough and waterproof

HERO

SPIDERMONKEY

Spidermonkey is an agile, chattering alien. He can stick to walls and create spider webs as tough as steel cable.

Ultimate

Ultimate HUMUNGOUSAUR

Even bigger and stronger than Humungousaur, Ultimate Humungousaur's back is covered by a large spiked shell, and he has a spiked ball on the end of his tail.

FACT FILE

- Formed when Swampfire hits his Omnitrix symbol
- Incredibly tough
- Can fire missiles from his hands

HUMUNGOUSAUR

Humungousaur is huge and powerful. He has thick dinosaur skin and can make his body grow up to an amazing 18 metres in height.

Ultimate CANNONBOLT

Like Cannonbolt, Ultimate Cannonbolt is covered in natural armour plating – but his Ultimate form is tougher and faster than ever.

FACT FILE

- Formed when Cannonbolt hits his Omnitrix symbol
- Immensely strong
- His webs are tough and waterproof

CANNONBOLT

Cannonbolt is a bulky alien whose body armour protects him from extreme heat. He can curl up into a ball to protect himself from attack.

Ultimate

31

Ultimate BIG CHILL

Ultimate Big Chill can breathe ice and produce ice flames – fire so cold that it burns. He can also shoot flames from his hands.

FACT FILE

- Formed when Big Chill hits his Omnitrix symbol
- Survives extreme cold and heat and even under water
- Can become invisible and fly super fast

BIG CHILL

Big Chill is capable of breathing a freezing vapour that can trap any of his targets in a thick layer of ice.

Ultimate ECHO ECHO

Ultimate Echo Echo is a noisy guy! He can shoot out floating discs from his body to create powerful sonic blasts – enough to knock an enemy out.

HERO

FACT FILE

- Formed when Echo Echo hits his Omnitrix symbol

- His sonic screams are enough to shatter steel

- Flies fast enough to create a deadly sonic boom

ECHO ECHO

He may be small, but Echo Echo can make as many exact copies of himself as he likes!

HOW TO DRAW
HEATBLAST

Draw lines for Heatblast's body and circles for his head, hands and feet.

1

3

TOP TIP
To make it easier, just trace round the big picture of Heatblast then fill in the details.

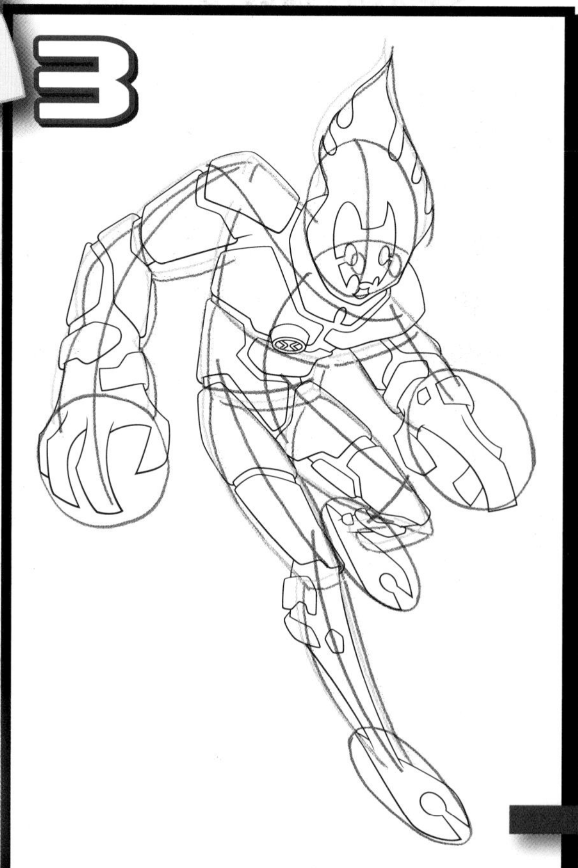

Now for the fun part! Draw all the heat plates on Heatblast's body. Remember that he only has four fingers and two toes!

2

Now add lines around the body so that Heatblast starts to take shape. Draw the flame on his head and his eyes — note that his eyes are quite low down on his head.

Once you're happy with your drawing, go over the lines in a black felt-tip pen. Erase all the unwanted lines and add some colour.

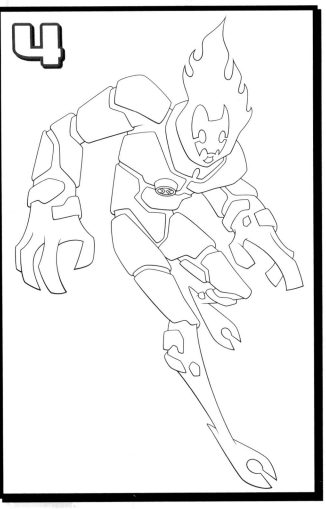

4

Answers on page 67.

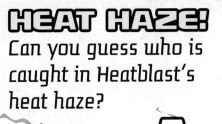

Can you guess who is caught in Heatblast's heat haze?

A

Write your answer here!

B

Write your answer here!

C

Write your answer here!

D

Write your answer here!

Ultimate Humungousaur is a mighty beast. Give him some colour and bring him to life!

SHE'S RIGHT, BEN. YOU RELY ON THE ULTIMATRIX TOO MUCH.

BUT I'VE GOT THIS POWER, GRANDPA. WHAT GOOD IS IT IF I DON'T USE IT?

POWER CAN BE A CRUTCH. AND IF YOU LEAN ON IT TOO MUCH--LIKE I LEAN ON SALT TO SAVE MY CHILI-- IT'LL ONLY HURT YOU IN THE END.

THERE'S SOMEONE I WANT YOU TO MEET. SMARTER GUY THAN I'LL EVER BE. AND I'LL HOLD ON TO THE ULTIMATRIX UNTIL YOU GET BACK.

BUT...

continued on page 50 ...

BAD GUYS

In the beginning, there was VILGAX, a vicious alien warlord who wanted the Omnitrix to help him conquer the galaxy.

STATUS: DEFEATED

DR. ANIMO is a villain who keeps returning to haunt Ben. He uses a device on his head to mutate animals into bigger and more dangerous versions of themselves.

STATUS: ACTIVE

Kevin used to be an all-out baddy! KEVIN 11 was one of Ben's main enemies, and one day he managed to absorb Ben's alien heroes.

STATUS: REFORMED

The HIGHBREED were a massive threat who wanted to cleanse the universe of everyone except themselves – and Earth was their next target.

STATUS: DEFEATED

The DNALIENS were the faceless and loyal servants to the HighBreed. They were created by attaching a facehugger-like parasite to the head of any human.

STATUS: DEFEATED

The FOREVER KNIGHTS are a constant threat to Ben. They wear a complete suit of metal body armour and seek alien technology for their own power.

STATUS: ACTIVE

AGGREGOR is the most dangerous villain Ben has ever met. He has kidnapped five aliens from their home planets in order to absorb their energy. These superpowers will help him gain ultimate domination of the universe ...

STATUS: **ACTIVE**

ZOMBOZO is a scary clown who just won't leave Ben alone! His weapons include steel streamers, an extending arm and an electric trick buzzer.

STATUS: **ACTIVE**

CHARMCASTER is a witch who can perform magic. She also has a team of tough rock monsters under her control.

STATUS: **ACTIVE**

VULKANUS is a tiny alien inside a large mechanical suit. He uses his huge laser blaster and has small but deadly 'pickaxe aliens' working for him.

STATUS: **ACTIVE**

WHICH SUPERHERO

Which of Ben's ULTIMATE aliens would be best to cope with each situation? Write down the alien name in the spaces.

1. Ben needs to heat up, then freeze some baddies.

_____

2. Ben wants to throw some fireballs.

_____

3. Ben needs to escape by rolling down a hill.

_____

4. Ben wants to trap some Forever Knights in a web.

_____

ECHO ECHOED

ECHO ECHO

Ultimate ECHO ECHO

Check out these alien shadows. Can you identify each one? Write their names in the spaces.

A

_ _ _ _ _ _ _ _ _ _ _

B

_ _ _ _ _ _ _ _ _ _ _

C

D

_ _ _ _ _ _ _ _

_ _ _ _ _ _ _ _

_ _ _ _ _ _ _ _ _ _ _

_ _ _ _ _ _ _ _ _ _ _

E

F

_ _ _ _ _ _ _ _

_ _ _ _ _ _ _ _

_ _ _ _ _ _ _ _ _ _ _

ANGRY AGGREGOR

Aggregor has sent his robot drones a cryptic message. Using the codebreaker, can you reveal Aggregor's sinister order?

6·9·14·4   2·5·14

20·5·14·14·25·19·15·14!

1	2	3	4	5	6	7	8	9
A	B	C	D	E	F	G	H	I

10	11	12	13	14	15	16	17	18
J	K	L	M	N	O	P	Q	R

19	20	21	22	23	24	25	26
S	T	U	V	W	X	Y	Z

Answer on page 68.

NEW DNA

Aggregor has kidnapped five aliens from across the galaxy and he wants to absorb all of their powers. Ben, Gwen and Kevin are trying to help the aliens and get them back to their home planets. But before they part, the Ultimatrix scans each of the aliens, giving Ben five brand new alien choices! Meet them here ...

Water Hazard has a tough shell like a crab, and he can shoot very powerful water jets from his hands.

Turtle-like **Terraspin** can spin and generate high-speed winds to confuse the enemy.

NRG is a red-hot life form encased in armour. He can shoot energy beams through his helmet.

Armodrillo is very strong and has drills for arms. He can create earthquakes.

Ampfibian is a jellyfish-like alien that can fire electrical bursts, drain electricity and become invisible.

NUMBER RESCUE

The DNAliens are on the attack and Gwen's magical orbs are failing. Can you show Kevin the quickest path to Gwen before it's too late? It's the route with the smallest total when the numbers are added together.

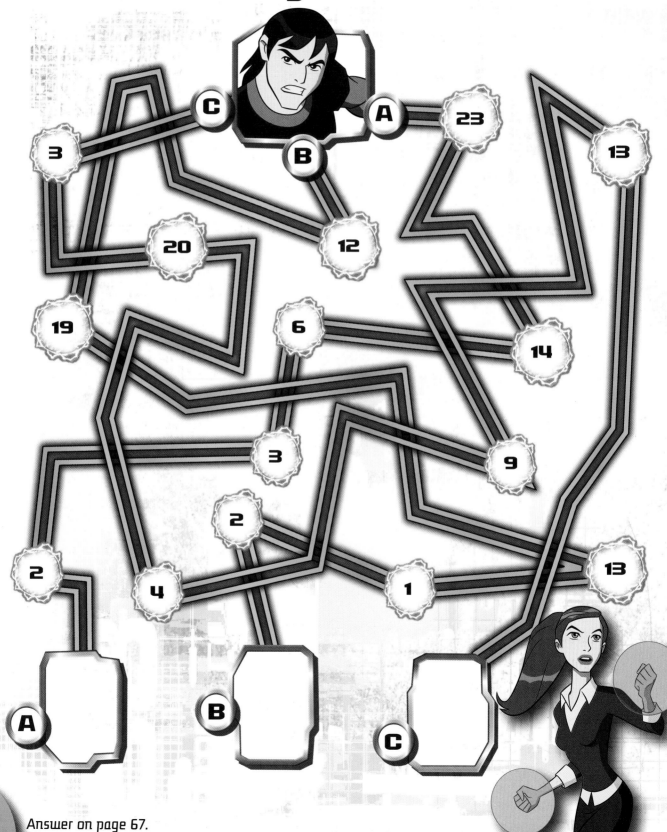

Answer on page 67.

3D SEARCH

There are heaps of aliens hanging out in this grid. Use your super vision to find them all! They can read down or across.

H	U	M	U	N	G	O	U	S	A	U	R	O	T	F	S
C	H	R	O	M	A	S	T	O	N	E	P	L	K	C	W
M	P	R	A	L	I	E	N	X	R	C	F	S	P	A	A
D	L	A	B	T	W	T	E	R	R	A	S	P	I	N	M
I	M	M	K	H	A	T	G	E	T	R	F	I	N	N	P
A	N	P	J	E	T	R	A	Y	C	M	P	D	R	O	F
M	B	F	A	B	E	K	D	G	O	O	P	E	T	N	I
O	D	I	C	R	R	T	S	F	D	D	U	R	G	B	R
N	H	B	T	A	H	B	C	B	F	R	T	M	G	O	E
D	W	I	C	I	A	R	A	T	H	I	N	O	Y	L	T
H	D	A	T	N	Z	F	P	Q	B	L	M	N	D	T	A
E	T	N	B	S	A	C	E	T	O	L	C	K	T	Y	F
A	V	D	E	T	R	A	M	L	E	O	D	E	M	P	C
D	F	G	L	O	D	E	S	T	A	R	H	Y	R	L	O
F	G	T	I	R	P	Y	C	E	C	H	O	E	C	H	O
U	L	T	I	M	A	T	E	B	I	G	C	H	I	L	L

Ultimate Big Chill

Spidermonkey

Rath

Humungousaur

Swampfire

Ampfibian

Diamondhead

Armodrillo

Alien X

ChromaStone

Terraspin

Goop

Cannonbolt

Water Hazard

Brain Storm

Echo Echo

Lodestar

Jet Ray

Answers on page 67.

HEATBLAST

Heatblast was Ben's very first alien transformation! Heatblast is one hot guy. He can aim bolts of fire from his hands and mouth and create fireballs for weapons. When he's angry, he can throw flames everywhere.

UPGRADE

Upgrade is a smooth mover. With skin made from liquid metal, he's able to merge into machines and travel along wires. He can upgrade any machine and can also fire a plasma beam from his eye.

WAY BIG

Way Big is Ben's most powerful alien! He's also the tallest, standing 200 feet high. He has incredible strength and is resistant to most attacks. He can also create energy blasts from his hands.

BENMUMMY

Benmummy is pretty creepy! He can control his many bandages, using them as tentacles, and he can also split them apart to dodge attacks and then reform. Benmummy can also recover from any injury – including being torn to pieces!

WAY BIG

EYEGUY

Eyeguy is the all-seeing alien. His whole upper body is covered in eyes – and from these, he can fire energy and freezing beams. Also, by merging every eye into one single massive one in his chest, he can fire a single huge energy blast!

HERO

WILDVINE

Wildvine is Ben's awesome green-fingered plant alien. His arms and legs are vines which he's able to grow or stretch. He can also grow thorns, merge with other plants, dig underground, and he has seeds on his back that can be used as explosives.

RATH

Angry by name, angry by nature! Rath is feisty and quick to get into a fight. He's also one of the most powerful aliens, able to lift and throw massive objects. He has a vicious, sharp claw on each wrist – perfect for shredding things.

LODESTAR

Lodestar is really magnetic! He has a tough body with a floating head held in place magnetically. He can also create magnetic fields and can repel, attract and send out magnetic pulses – allowing him to control metallic objects.

GOOP

Goop is a gloopy, shape-shifting green blob! Made of slime, Goop controls his movements through a small UFO that floats above his head. He can form his body into any position, allowing an easy way out of sticky situations.

NANOMECH

Nanomech is a carbon-based life form who comes from a hive of insects. He's already tiny, but he's able to make himself even smaller – handy for spying, sneaking around and even climbing inside complex machinery!

FOUR ARMS

Four Arms is a handy guy and is Ben's favourite alien! At 12 feet high, he has almighty strength and can create shockwaves by pounding the ground or clapping all four of his hands together. His legs are so strong, he can cross entire cities in a single jump.

DIAMONDHEAD

Diamondhead is a razor-sharp guy, made from extremely hard crystals. He's able to cut and slash through anything and he can fire crystal shards from his body. He can re-grow lost limbs and bounce energy attacks off his crystal body.

NAME GAME

Take the letters shown from the names of each of these aliens. Use those letters to spell out the name of another alien.

1 — 9th letter
CANNONBOLT

2 — 4th letter
NANOMECH

3 — 5th letter
ARMODRILLO

4 — 4th letter
ALIEN X

5 — 1st letter
SWAMPFIRE

6 — 7th letter
BRAIN STORM

7 — 2nd letter
RATH

8 — 5th letter
WATER HAZARD

The alien is:

___ ___ ___ ___ ___ ___ ___ ___
1   2   3   4   5   6   7   8

ALIEN FRIENDS

Check out these alien notes, then match them up with people you know. One of them could be you!

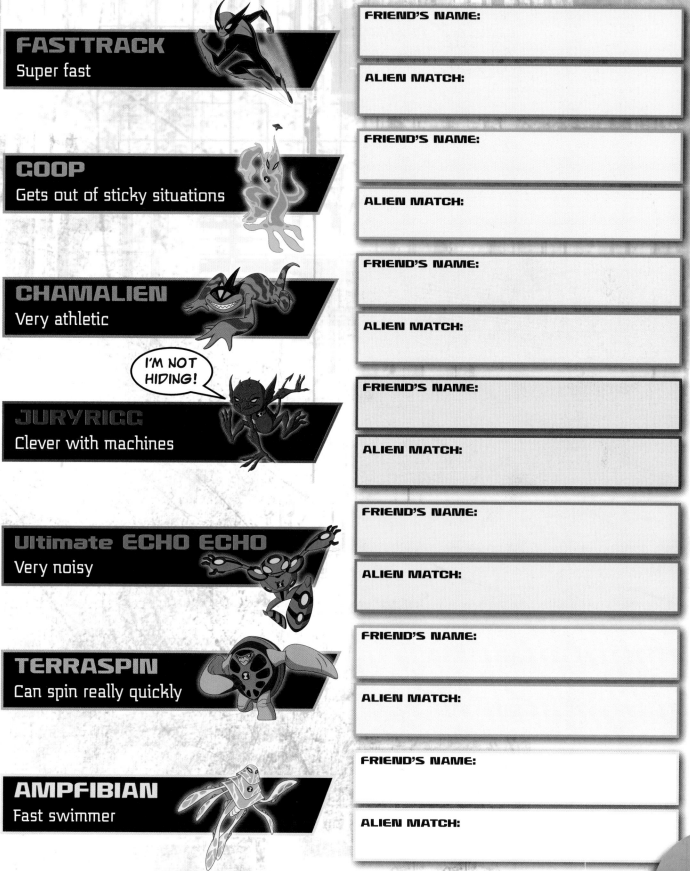

FASTTRACK
Super fast

FRIEND'S NAME:

ALIEN MATCH:

GOOP
Gets out of sticky situations

FRIEND'S NAME:

ALIEN MATCH:

CHAMALIEN
Very athletic

FRIEND'S NAME:

ALIEN MATCH:

I'M NOT HIDING!

JURYRIGG
Clever with machines

FRIEND'S NAME:

ALIEN MATCH:

Ultimate ECHO ECHO
Very noisy

FRIEND'S NAME:

ALIEN MATCH:

TERRASPIN
Can spin really quickly

FRIEND'S NAME:

ALIEN MATCH:

AMPFIBIAN
Fast swimmer

FRIEND'S NAME:

ALIEN MATCH:

BYE, HEROES!

Add some colour to our ULTIMATE HERO. You could even draw yourself next to Ben!

THANKS, GUYS. SEE YOU AGAIN SOON!

ANSWERS

Page 11
DANGER MAZE

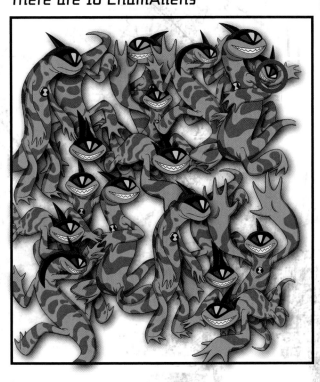

Page 13
CHAMALIEN COUNT
There are 16 ChamAliens

Page 17
MOMENT IN TIME

Page 35
HEAT HAZE
A – Kevin 11, B – Grandpa Max,
C – Dr. Animo, D – Gwen.

Page 41
GWEN'S TEST
Gwen should take path C.

Page 45
WHICH SUPERHERO?
1 – Ultimate Big Chill, 2 – Ultimate
Swampfire, 3 – Ultimate Cannonbolt,
4 – Ultimate Spidermonkey.

ECHO ECHOED
Echo Echo appears 16 times,
Ultimate Echo Echo 14 times.

Page 46
ANGRY AGGREGOR
Find Ben Tennyson.

Page 47
ALIEN ID
A – Ampfibian, B – Lodestar,
C – Ultimate Big Chill,
D – Ultimate Swampfire,
E – Ultimate Echo Echo,
F – Armodrillo.

Page 56
NUMBER RESCUE
Kevin should take path B.

Page 57
3D SEARCH

H	U	M	U	N	G	O	U	S	A	U	R	O	T	F	S
C	H	R	O	M	A	S	T	O	N	E	P	L	K	C	W
M	P	R	A	L	I	E	N	X	R	C	F	S	P	A	A
D	L	A	B	T	W	T	E	R	R	A	S	P	I	N	M
I	M	M	K	H	A	T	G	E	T	R	F	I	N	N	P
A	N	P	J	E	T	R	A	Y	C	M	P	D	R	O	F
M	B	F	A	B	E	K	D	G	O	O	P	E	T	N	I
O	D	I	C	R	R	T	S	F	D	D	U	R	G	B	R
N	H	B	T	A	H	B	C	B	F	R	T	M	G	O	E
D	W	I	C	I	A	R	A	T	H	I	N	O	Y	L	T
H	D	A	T	N	Z	F	P	Q	B	L	M	N	D	T	A
E	T	N	B	S	A	C	E	T	O	L	C	K	T	Y	F
A	V	D	E	T	R	A	M	L	E	O	D	E	M	P	C
D	F	G	L	O	D	E	S	T	A	R	H	Y	R	L	O
F	G	T	I	R	P	Y	C	E	C	H	O	E	C	H	O
U	L	T	I	M	A	T	E	B	I	G	C	H	I	L	L

Page 64
NAME GAME
The alien is Lodestar.

Juryrigg is hiding on pages 12, 18, 23, 27, 34, 47, 54, 59, 64 and 67.

ADVERTISEMENT